CROWN ANTHOLOGY

CROWN ANTHOLOGY

LOST POETS

Edited by Analog de Léon & Gabriel Sage

Andrews McMeel
PUBLISHING®

For the lost.

Foreword

I think poetry and I see Whitman, roaming a countryside long since gone, notebook in hand, I see the words. I think poetry and I see Bukowski, smoke-stained, bearded, dimly lit and leaned in, I see the words. I think poetry and I see Neruda, I see Cummings, Eliot, Dickinson, Plath, I see Brautigan, Ginsberg, Kerouac, I see Maya Angelou throwing hope like a promise, I see Sarah Kay's lyricism, Ada Limón's tangible earthiness, I see Billy Collins and Jim Harrison, and still, I see the words.

We are united by words, and we've always been. For far too long, the world felt far too big, and the only words we found were those close enough to be whispered, or if we were monumentally lucky, those that were handed to us in a worn-out book, dog-eared and bent in half, back pocket folded and creased from overuse. For far too long those words, that poetry, seemed to be fading into memory, an art form dying, the death rattle of a medium that has always felt vital to the fabric of the human condition. And then, a long deep breath, and lungs refilled.

I think poetry and I see scraps of paper indented from old typewriters, the ghosting of letters pressed harder than the rest, if only slightly, if only randomly. I see an ocean of creativity spread across a shrinking planet, I see arms linked and passion shared and a community growing. I see the words. Some time ago, I'm not positive when, poetry started drumming instead of rattling, it started thumping wildly against its own fading, it started mattering again. I browse poetry sections in bookstores across the world on my travels now, and I am bombarded with new names, new covers, new faces filling new author photo frames on the back covers, I see the words.

We are words, those we write, those we read, and those taking root inside us. We are the blossoming of them into sentences, into verse, into lyric and rhythm, we are their petals dropping and blowing across the landscapes that may separate us. We are the words, these within, and all those not yet leaked onto page or screen; we are the words, the importance of them, and the shared knowledge that someone, somewhere, feels the same as we do.

I think poetry and I think of the singing of our aches. These aches, those, and all of them to come. Still, I see the words.

—Tyler Knott Gregson

INTRODUCTION

"My crown is called content, a crown that
seldom kings (and queens) enjoy."
—Shakespeare

Crown Anthology is a book of community and hope, created
from the singular idea that great art has the power to unite. It
was birthed in the voices of an online poetry subculture, along
the internet alleyways of social media and within the electronic
exchanges of hundreds of poets and artisans.

As cofounders of Lost Poets, we have seen for ourselves the
power of community. It can be the stone in a turbulent riverbed
and a breaker that hardship and loneliness can't stand against.
Crown Anthology began as a community project to provide
hope for a subculture of poets recovering from a trying time of
hopelessness and lost dreams. And while it is easy to linger in
any tide of darkness, we have chosen to instead write about what
grew back despite the flood.

Crown Anthology is a story about hope and restoration. It
affirms that every soul is royal and tells the timeless story we
will hopefully all get a chance to experience in our lifetime—
the path from separation to wholeness, the journey to find our
crown amidst the brokenness of the world.

Stand anywhere in the world right now, on any continent, in any city or capital, on top of any mountain, and the reality is that there is nowhere without injustice, without the hopeless, the helpless, or the broken. More than ever there is a global recognition of disharmony in the hearts of humans, but as the midnight of our time looms ominous in the future, hope is still an anchor.

Over recent years, a great resurgence in the art of words has enveloped the modern globe. Poetry has not been so widely popular since Ginsberg and the Beat Generation wrote the rhythm at the heart of their time into the pages of the global consciousness.

In the wake of this movement in modern poetry, a gritty and impassioned subculture formed. *Crown Anthology* is the culmination of one hundred of those artists joined together with the common goal to use their art for healing and hope. Each of the gifted authors add their own story and voice to affirm themes of love and loss, hope and restoration, lending to *Crown Anthology* a blend of diversity and empowerment through the lens of every race, gender, and culture, with contributors joining from nearly every major country across the globe.

O'Lost. O'Found.

INTRODUCTION

Every great tide of change began with a simple action, every great odyssey a single step. Our journey begins with O'Found. An idea more than a series, O'Found recognizes the ability for art to entrench the ills of the world with perspective and harmony. If it ignites thought, provokes action, or inspires hope, it is O'Found. Pressed into the opening pages of a book or on the corner of a canvas, O'Found is a watermark for art in resistance; it connects artists and poets from all walks of life with a singular silver cord, a shared DNA of hope.

O'Found is a sigil for poets and musicians, artists and revolutionaries—a means to assert voice and intention into the eternal conversation of love and living.

O'Found is the mark of *purpose*.

In November of 2017, *Vertigo,* by Analog de Lēon, was published to inaugurate the O'Found series. The mission of O'Found and the idea behind the book coalesce to initiate our ethos of resistance. *Vertigo* is a book about climbing onto the rooftop of the world and standing down a great tide of darkness, a modern epic about a lost poet in retrograde twenty-two thousand miles above the skyline in defiance. It tells a story, laced with luminous layers of silk, symbol, and allegory, about the turbulence of letting go, being present, and rising up.

INTRODUCTION

The second O'Found release, in the summer of 2018, was a record by troubadour and poet Jess Adams. The album, *Riverstone*, speaks to the tumultuous cycles of life that turn walls of jaded reservations into open spaces of vulnerability. It is about finding yourself in the vastness, about the rough edges of life, smoothed by the river, Lost.

The third, *Heart & Stone*, by Gabriel Sage, is a book of poetry that examines the modern metropolitan world in all its beautiful sludge and wild truth. Holding a mirror to the vogue, it is about the complexities and anxieties that shroud contemporary life. From the winding alleys and bright lights of the city through the twisting winds in the bosom of the high desert, the story of a generation unfolds in a search for solid ground among the elusive clouds.

This book, *Crown Anthology*, continues the tradition. A poetry anthology dedicated to self-love and empowerment, to rising out of darkness and finding our way home.

Today, our community of Lost Poets is meeting, delving, grinding away in digital basements all across the world, carefully placing one more word on the page and one more wrench in the machine. Each age has its own unique challenges, but one thing remains the same: Art has the power to shake people out of apathy and into action. Art and literature can make impact in ways that no other influence can, and for the writers collected in camaraderie across these pages, this book is our proof.

Can words really make a difference? It's not enough to talk about love. We must become love.

—Gabriel Sage & Analog de Lēon (Chris Purifoy)

Contents

Foreword . . . . *v*
Introduction . . . . *vii*

Tender Is the Night 1

Paradise Lost 41

As I Lay Dying 77

The Sun Also Rises 117

Look Homeward, Angel . . . 165

About the Authors 215
An Open Letter to the Lost . . 217
Artist Index 219
Acknowledgments 223
About Lost Poets 225

TENDER IS THE NIGHT

They say we should learn
to love ourselves before we love another,
but I wasn't taught how to do either.

When you don't know
how to receive,
even giving looks like taking.
The affection isn't liberation;
it's conspiracy.
Trojan words of war
disguised as compromise.

Then, even loving feels like losing.

—*Christopher Ferreiras*

Speak Heavy

Speak heavy to me—
long, stocky words,
thick syllables,
thumping every letter
with haughty breaths.

Let me know your
deepest thoughts,
your most complex
wonderings.
Sound them out
clearly,
powerfully,
to my listening ears.

—*Topher Kearby*

One day I will meet a girl.

She will be the ocean,
and I will sail every inch of her expanse.
I will leave poems on her pillow in the morning.
I will leave sonnets on her skin in the evening.
I will always find ways to hold her hand,
beneath every table,
on every walk,
during every moment.

She will go to bed at night
certain of her beauty.
She will wake up in the morning
convinced of her value.

She will have a key
to explore the endless recesses
of my mind and heart—
I will open every door for her.

I will write with her a story
that makes Shakespeare proud,

even the sun and moon
will take notice and be jealous.

One day I will meet a girl.

—*Analog de Lēon*

We are all mad here.
But I stand next to you,
naked and poor,
madly in love.

—*Richard A. Camus*

Maybe I just want
to live as though
we're the first
to baptize
the streets of
New York
with a love
        so grand
we'd barter
our dollar dreams
against a night
        in Hell
if it meant pressing
my hips against
yours the next
morning.

—*Alice Morrison*

I am
balancing
delicately
on the cusp
of wanting you
and needing you

that line I scratch
so deeply in the dust
is unsettling
as I am in myself

with every part of me
standing on end for you

begging
upon your hands
to be laid flat.

—*Lauren Eden*

This is not a poem.

Today I was approached by a complete stranger while walking my dog. She said that hers had passed away a season ago. She's woken up at the same time every morning since and walked the same path they walked together for 14 years. She said that she misses him, but finds comfort in their routine.

This is not a poem.
The love in her sadness was.

—Patrick Hart

it is fearful, but we crave new beginnings.

know I want to read in the silence of the library
that belongs to only our collective hands.

you will prop your feet up on my two legs
and we will drift through worlds
while never moving anything but pages.

do you hear that in the distance? the echoing siren?
the sailor's call? the warning?

i barely do anymore. (you are my world.)

i move nothing if I have not moved you.
it is true, I am consumed by love.

but the language of this place has always been a little
maddened.

do you hear that in the distance?
is it not a downpour? radio static? tree roots unwinding?
is it not the kind of rain that washes away?

maybe the light has come to apologize for
leaving, but all the anecdotes become leeches on its
tongue;
i can hide nothing through the window.

it even looks a little new. a little like a beginning.

you will not bat an eye.
your fingers will trace the line on the page in front of you.

'and if it is not me you are running to let the running be the quickest route to freedom. and if your legs decide to carry you to me, let our love never feel like quicksand.'

(you are my world.)

—*Alison Malee*

We do this thing, we talk without talking.
  Reading our bodies, page by page, exchanging
  mannerisms instead of words.

We do this thing, we look without looking.
  Evading contact, eyes up and down, taking pictures
  with our minds.

We do this thing, we touch without touching.
  Grazing while passing, skin on skin, pretending it's
  accidental.

We do this thing, we dance without dancing.
  Colliding feet, leading and following, unknowingly
  performing a waltz.

We do this thing, we fight without fighting.
  Pushing far away, cold and stoic, striking distance
  escapes us.

We do this thing, we feel without feeling.
  Abandoning our emotions, thrusting and grinding,
  longing only in bed.

We do this thing, we love without loving.
  Effortlessly giving, anything and everything, acting as
  if it all means nothing.

—*Vivi Dale*

Marrow

My bones are stifled in more than my own skin now.
They are stifled within your skin too—
in the crevices of your smile
and the soft tissue of your weary limbs.
Because when I say I love you,
it means I am no longer living just for myself,
but for you, your nightmares and your dreams too.

—*Allison Theresa*

I accidentally swallowed
a smile and breathed
straight into its mouth.
A butterfly flew
down my throat
and settled in my gut.
My vision was blurry and
a cat combed my hair.
The ceiling had fingermarks
and love was just a drug.

—*R. X. Bird*

Deserve

I don't dare
Question
What I did to
Deserve you—
That would suggest
I don't believe
That I do.
I express gratitude,
Instead,
For your coming
Into my life
At a time when I knew
What I deserved.

—*J. Bird*

I can assure you that,
without its thorns,
the rose would not be quite as beautiful as it is.
The very fact that something
so delicate, pure, sublime, and immaculate
has contrast in its character—
sharp edges that can draw blood—
make roses worthy of adoration.
And this is the problem with most people—
they all demand beauty,
but hardly any of them
are bold enough to hold it.

—*Daniel Saint*

Love me loud like clanking bottles
tied to a galloping horse, and when
they shatter I will pick up every
single piece of glass so we don't
have to watch our step. Or would
you rather tread amongst these
fragments like eggshells and pretend
you aren't bleeding, but you'd be a
fool to think I don't care enough to
notice. My faith matches the
highness of which I carry your name
and how I look for it in everything
like a star amidst the daylight, like
happiness in my wildest dreams.

—*Anthony Desmond*

Her skin was the canvas for a new day—
I knew as I touched every particle of her body.
Her mouth, the oxygen to breathe—
as I kissed her over and over.
Those beautiful eyes contained the colors
to stop seeing life in black and white.

—*Richard A. Camus*

Let me hold your hurt
and quiet the petulant aches that reign your moods.
Let me look upon you with my love-soaked eyes
and absorb every piece of your beauty.
Let me fortify the deficiency of unanswered desires
and feed you an abundance of lust.
Let me love you with the tenderness of my touch
and drench your desiccated body
with the rainfall of my affection.
Let me give you everything you seek and deserve,
because we both know,
she never will.

—*Vivi Dale*

A Grander Life

We took cheap wine
up the mountain, sat with
our legs dangling from its
face and pretended we lived
a grander life in the city
below our feet.
For those few hours,
I felt like everything was okay,
with you in my arms and
cheap wine on our lips.

—*Daniel Walsh*

Eternity

I'll love you for eternity.
That's what we all say.
We say that our hearts will
still be beating
for only each other
even after we both decay
and turn to ash.
How cliché.

Before death,
my last emotion will be
adoration for you.
This adoration, my darling,
will flow into our universe
and create this new life—
our soil will grow
new trees and daffodils.

I might not be able to promise
a love for eternity,
but when I'm gone

you will find my love
in the nearest baby willow tree—
ever-growing.

—*Sica Saccone*

Evolution

It is remarkable,
The evolution of self.
The normalization of a situation.
How these two
Progressions
Can run parallel to one another
And never quite meet.

In times when I would be
Free of trouble,
I would stagnate.
Possibly regress.
It is in times of hardship
Or challenge, however, when
I
Become.

In the face of anger,
I seek peace.
In the face of entitlement, of loss,
I seek gratitude.
In the face of ignorance,
I seek knowledge.
In the face of unkindness,
I seek empathy.

—*J. Bird*

He somehow makes
eternity make sense.
I'm not sure
if I believe
in love
at first sight.

All I know
is that
the second my eyes
met his,
I started counting
to infinity.

—*Cindy Cherie*

Wait
until
it
feels
like
home.

—*Analog de Lēon*

If you ever forget
what love looks like,
go watch the arrival gates
at the airport.
Go see day-old flowers
on decade-old tombstones,
or a man sitting on a bench
sharing a cannoli with
his dog.
Listen to a song.
Admire a painting.

Love is literally everywhere.

—*Michael Layao*

My happiness lies in yours.
So, in the future if it turns out
that I am crazily, madly,
irrevocably in love with you
but you don't feel the same
way, I will let go for you.
Even though it will absolutely
kill me on the inside. Even
though I might be broken
to the point of no return,
I will let you go for you.
Because my happiness lies
in your happiness.

—*a paradox.*

—*Ruby Dhal*

Still

I rub the sleep from my eyes
and stumble hazily out of bed.

I twist the blinds open,
put some water on the stove,
and take the silkiest of throws out of the cabinet.

I crawl back in bed and prop myself up
on the old wooden headboard.

Still,
it is not the sun I feel filtering through the panels,
not the warm tea running into my stomach,
and not the cashmere on my skin that is it.

Still,
the light, warmth, and softness I am feeling
comes from the body sleeping messy and quiet
next to me.

—*N. Wong*

The sky
   is full of the moon
  and my head
   is full of you.
I melt for you.
I surrender to you.
I want your grip on my hips
  and bruises left on my skin
   in the shape
  of your fingertips.

—*Natalie Jensen*

She is my
wonderland,
and I can't
ask for more.

And he is the
rabbit hole
I'd tumble
through over
and over for.

—*Richard A. Camus and Raquel Franco*

if i lie still on my back
my stomach will howl and gurgle
and it doesn't ever stop
i have always been full of noise
and there are hollows
wee crescent moons at the base of my spine
like thumb prints

there are a dozen small things that make
a good poem
and none of them are really talents
or grammar
mostly just inhaling the words
falling in love with the person in them
and
realizing it is you.

—*featherdownsoul*

Storm

She is the shred of light
I need in my charcoal nights,
the lightning of my storm.
Against all my better judgment,
I always hope she will electrify me . . .
just once.

—*Sica Saccone*

Synthetic

Suddenly, hands over your face—
coffee steams from a white mug on the table—
closed on one side,
a bartender gave us a quiet place
to visit.

In silence I stare
under yellow lights.

Tears fall from wrists, elbows on stomach,
wrinkles on fingers, drops glisten
on black down jacket,

heat dissolves past hairline—
strands of yarn pasted on canvas.
A metal shard forms the chair's back.
Fruit peels creased, coated in wax, tar smeared
below skin—charcoal shapes breasts and waist—
melted Styrofoam.

—*Chase Maser*

I need your arms,
not your words.

—*Vivi Dale*

I'm questioning the validity
of the ground beneath me.
You see, I'm falling for you,
for the soft behind your eyes.
I'm lost in the corners of your smile
and the waves crashing in your hair,
languishing and drifting away to somewhere high,
an altitude from where I don't want to come down,
from where I don't even try.
This is what it means to be swept away.

—A.R. Asher

Our hearts cannot grow stronger
without knowing the feeling of pain.
Just as wildflowers cannot stand tall
without the showers of rain.

—*S.L. Gray*

I still remember the way
you used to hold my hands,
and how it was the only time
they ever stopped

s h aki n g.

—*Andrew Durst*

All I want
is something real,
something that is
terrifying to the touch
but far too beautiful
to ever let go of.

—*faraway*

When the workday has trampled over me—
bloody and bruised—
I come home to rub her feet . . .
for they would never tread on me.

—*C. Noel*

You know what breaks me?
When someone is visibly excited
about a feeling or an idea or a hope
or a risk taken, and they tell you about it
but preface it with: "Sorry, this is dumb but—".

Don't do that.

I don't know who came here before me,
who conditioned you to think
you had to apologize or feel obtuse.
But not here. Dream so big it's silly.
Laugh so hard it's obnoxious.
Love so much it's impossible.

And don't you ever feel,
unintelligent. And don't you ever
apologize. And don't you ever
shrink so you can squeeze yourself
into small places and small minds.

Grow. It's a big world. There's room.
You fit. I promise.

—*Owen Lindley*

Once Again

You're like déjà vu to me—
the new feels old.
The here and now feels like
a familiar there and then.

I've often wondered how much
fits in a first glance,
and I finally understood
the night we met.
It's in-between the words
and thoughts
and whiskey sips,
when perfect
becomes a tense of time.

You are this moment,
this moment is you,
and I feel like this has all happened before.

—*Gabriel Sage*

Find somebody for whom you're willing to grow.
Start with yourself.
Build yourself,
prove your worth to yourself,
support yourself,
value yourself,
and love yourself so much that
putting your heart back on the line again
doesn't feel like a risk
but, instead, feels like an opportunity
for love and self-love.

—*Horacio Jones*

Paradise Lost

someone once told me
the significance
of staying

only lasts as long
as there is
tenderness, too.

—*Alison Malee*

PARADISE LOST

They say gravity has a maximum speed—
as if we can only fall so fast and so hard.
I guess there is nothing new
in the way we collapse,
but I have stood on a mountain
as high as the moon,
then, with one blink,
found myself so low in the valley
that the skyline
was lost from view.
There is no limit
to the speed of falling love.

I fell for her in eight days.
It took years to climb back out of that hole.
I'm still scaling silver ladders from the chasm
as my thoughts collide with paper.

We fall in love and then fall from love.
Just once I want to love without falling.

—Analog de Léon

Anyone who has ever said
that silence is not deafening
has never heard her voice
and had to go without it.

—*Kate Foster*

Echo Skin

I cannot look
at my naked skin
anymore.
I cannot look at my body
without seeing
a skin
of tainted memories,
taut on top of mine.
My own palms repel from it—
every touch feels like his,
an echo
of all the times his hands
met it.
I await the day
this skin falls away,
when I feel beautiful
again.

—*N. Wong*

Letting go is a
mysterious place
often traveled
to alone.
You will show up
defeated, but
you will leave
with a brand new
sword.

—*Erin Van Vuren*

Like clouds,
your heart
breaks after
the storm.

You break like dawn
into the early morn.
You don't break in two;
you break into.
This is how you break free
and break through.

—*T. Weiss*

After Hours

"Babe, I feel restless," I whisper,
knowing you won't hear me
as you sleep by my side,
and I watch the ceiling fan playing games
with the shadows.
Let me tell you all the things
I've told the night
too many times before.

—*Gabriel Sage*

I Am in the Silences

I cannot control
My mouth.
When I want to say
The most important
Words,
My lips will not
Part,
My teeth are ivory bars
And will not let them out.

When I want to say
Nothing,
My tongue catapults
Words into the air,
Because soundlessness
Is so much more
Exposing
And I am wary
Of my own vulnerability.

Quiet me.
It is there that you will
Discover who I am.
I am in the silences.

—*J. Bird*

I am
always
surprised
when
someone
hurts me

no matter
how many times
I've been
hurt before

and I can't
seem to
work out

if that
is the definition
of innocence

or insanity.

—*Lauren Eden*

I was so drawn to you.
I felt as if
I was meant to find you,
but there's something
so uneasy about you and me.
So, if you look ahead
into your life,
and not seeing me
doesn't break your heart,
then I must have been
meant to lose you.

—*Natalie Jensen*

The Fragmented Soul

He was torn in half
Tormented at night
But made himself whole
With morning's first light;

Two sides
Held tight
Bound together
By lies.

—*Emilija Blum*

We chased infinity
as though our love
wasn't enough.
These days
I'm tired of running,
I've grown to love
the home
that we've built
in each other,
even if it's just
temporary.

—*Almaz A.*

Hairline Fracture

She is gone,
and all that
is left is
despair
and her hair
lined in the fabric
of everything
that I was.
All at once,
everything is
fractured.

— *T. Weiss*

You call me every now and then,
complaining of the remnants of
muddled bitters and orange sugars
on your tongue.
Nothing can quite wash me down,
but you can't quite have any seconds.

I indulge you as you settle for
the sound of my voice.
You salivate and imagine,
swallow and remember,
that old-fashioned love that is me.

At first taste,
she was exquisite—
the remedy for another long day,
caramel with a kick.
I drank her back too quickly,
like I needed every sip,
and I did.

So now the ice is melting
with what's left of the bitters,

and I'm missing that old-fashioned love
but ready for another drink.

—*Allison Theresa and Gabriel Sage*

I cling to summer
as it slips from my fingertips

dreams of you
swirl into my teacup

I take a sip
and try to ingest
the last traces of you

with the faintly lit summer
dancing away in hues of gold and rain

life reverts into its old fashion
comfortable
and safe

maybe I am ready
to let go of summer
because it means holding once again
totally
to you

—*Gabrielle Dufrene*

I wonder what your days are like now
and if they're anything like mine
daydreaming constantly
and staring at the skyline
when you get done with work
do you yell out, "Honey, I'm home"?
If you do, our days would differ,
in my home, I'm all alone.
Do you put your headphones on
and think about our past lives?
Or do you recycle all the things we said,
our favorite lyrics or movie lines?
And when you lie your head down at night,
do you count problems or sheep?
I've been counting everything but you
and to this day, I still can't sleep.

—*Leya Noir*

freedom is relative to where
you are and where you are not.
to where you have been and
the miles yet to go.
it's an elusive, curious mirage
i walk toward wondering
if the gap between the two
will ever be bridged.

—*angie allen*

The strings that suspend me
from heaven
are just strong enough
to keep me
from hell.
I am a tease to
the earth below me,
the ground would swallow me whole
if I fell.

—*Caroline White*

Then I am reminded
that I must live
and that I have no idea
what that means without her.

—*Christopher Ferreiras*

Small Talks

Within the borders of our fleeting conversation,
words bounce back and forth between us—
with no purpose,
direction or destination,
they get lost
under all the other voices.
Speaking about nothing.
Drinking about something.
Just one more word
before you leave
and blow cigarette smoke into the night.

—*Gabriel Sage*

Tomorrow

Endings are never simple.

There will be times when you won't be able to see
a tomorrow without someone in your todays,
but those days will pass and tomorrow will come . . .
for you are not defined by anyone but yourself,
and with time you will find that even the sharpest pains
can dull to nothing more than a distant ache.

Trust me when I say that
you will learn to live, love, and smile once again.

—*Becca Lee*

PARADISE LOST

I am moving on but stuck in reverse—
between the ears,
gumming up gears,
running through the years,
wondering how I ended my story on sour notes
on more than one occasion
by gnashing my teeth,
crying for one more chance to never let go of the past,
like a Christmas tree still lit up in July.

—The Poetry Bandit

A part of it was real
I think.
It had to be.
Because it didn't start from nothing;
you can't break nothing.

—*Kayil Crow*

Paradise Lost

Her eyes were ripe,
violet,
and hanging,
like bursting late autumn concords,
that, for no reason other than
the carelessness
of man,
remained yet unpicked.

Fools.

—*Michael Fawaz*

You shake me to my core with your hello,
and foolishly I inhale every word that comes after,
feeling them crawling their way down my lungs,
swimming through my veins,
making their way to my heart
to suffocate my arteries.
You had me at hello,
and I never stood a chance at breathing.

—*M. FireChild*

Paradise Lost

I am the last leaf
that hangs on
beyond fall
I outlast the
death of winter
and am still there
while the new buds
form in the spring
longing for just
one more summer.

—*stacie martin*

For once I'd like to strip myself of this imprinted billboard I've learned to plaster on the busiest street of my heart—that says, "Right person, wrong time."

—*Olivia Ku*

Paradise Lost

I know it is tiresome, my love,
to keep swinging your sledgehammer
at my facade
only to get a glimpse of what is inside.
But I was not always like this, you know?
They made me this way.
No one ever cared enough about my insides
to keep swinging.
So please do not stop.
I want you to ruin me.

—*Emina Gašpar-Vrana*

We are survivors—broken and defeated—
standing on a foreign shore.
Waves of the past crash over our feet,
washing away both sin and memory.
Come to where we are kings
and see our strength—
the place where time and shadows
aren't measured by length.

—*Adan Portwood*

Why sit with paupers
when you can stand with queens?
You've earned your royalty,
the purple regalia of your struggle
draped proudly across your shoulders.
You won't sit high on a throne
like others do.
You know what it's like
to beg in the streets,
to look up and see nothing but walls.
You will stand proud though
with your king at your side,
and always bow low
to help those who desire to rid themselves
of the chains they carry,
and trade them in for the
crown they've earned.

—*J. L. Wyman*

Don't allow the pains of your past
to grow on you like a phantom limb.
Use your ruins to build
beautiful kingdoms and castles,
rather than allowing them to tear you down.
I don't deserve it and neither do you.
Protect your soul.
Become its mate.
You are royalty.
We all are.

—*Soeline Bosari*

I held on until my hands
began to bleed . . .

My palms were scarred
and I no longer knew the
difference between my
lifelines and the
reminders you left upon
them . . .

—*A.D.Woods*

You are who you are,
and, no matter how hard you try
pretending to be whole,
I know you are a broken puzzle,
trying to find all the right pieces.
I honor that part of you
that yearns to be put back together.

—*Adrian Michael Green*

We hang like a chandelier
in an empty church.
Derelict and damned,
we are cursed
to have our lights burn
for no one.

—*The Poetry Bandit*

As I Lay Dying

Speaking

Silence speaks volumes—
of pages,
of chapters,
of novels,
of never-ending distance
placed between family,
between friends,
between lovers.

But words . . .
Oh, words, how clumsily they fall,
dislodging from your throat
in a tumbling, dizzying downpour
of vowels
and syllables
and mistakes.

Words
are sharper than the pinprick of a needle,
enough now.

hear me when i say,
heat escapes open mouths
even when you trust them.

the sun and the dawn
all exhale steady breaths.

and lips find
other lips
find other lips

find other
lips.

—*Alison Malee*

somethin' about
sharks and
lions
& pissed off
junkyard dogs

somethin' about
baring your
teeth
and letting them
gleam

somethin' about
lettin' the next
year know
you're human

but you fight
like somethin'
otherworldly

—*Jarod W.*

As I Lay Dying

I don't think I could ever be a great writer.
I can't be honest enough
when I write on these paper walls.
So much of me is hidden
beneath a veneer of strength
that isolates me from everyone.

Being strong
has always helped me build
communities for other people,
but almost no one really knows why
I sometimes wake up breathless
and waste entire days
trying to catch it again.

My father told me
we connect in our weakness
not our strength.
I can't stop thinking about that.

—*Analog de Lēon*

You may know your worth,
but that doesn't mean you value it.

—*Horacio Jones*

As I Lay Dying

What's to be made of sea and silt,

of obstruction,
of the porous and eroding?

What of an indisposed Atlantic coast,

left with nothing,
nothing but names,

naively engraved
though permanence has no favor
here among the drifts?

I have taken a tally of fingers
in their tasting the wind,

felt coercion as a passerby,
to move,
to follow,
to heed,

yet the bottoms of my feet are rough
from this directionless roaming.

I have whispered breathy sonnets
in smoke-filled exhalations of wild plumes,

risen with the rapid nature of currents,
to seek,
to speak to hope,

yet even still coal is not of my makeup,

to shrivel just to be desired,
to be fuel,
to be consumed.

What's to be made of
fire and ember?

of discord?
of what is left dry?

I will not be left to burn.

—*Sarah Maria*

Plucked

You give me wings
just to pluck each feather
from my back
and watch me crash
back to earth.

—*Topher Kearby*

I am more than warm flesh. The scarred skin that covers my organs and cushions my bones wasn't meant for anything more. That sway in my hips is nothing more than something I was forced to learn when I barely knew how to walk.

I am more than the wintry-ocean blue swimming in my eyes. That glint is nothing more than panic. That wide-eyed expression is nothing more than fear.

I am more than the breath in my lungs. A vessel to break and belittle. I was born with lungs meant to breathe air and a voice that is meant to be heard, not stifled.

I am intelligence—capable of making up my own mind. I am heart—loving as hard as I can on the ones that matter. I am soul—caring, gentle.

I am more than the pain I've endured. I am more than what you made out of me. I am everything you never could be.

And I bet that's not something you expected.

—*Sarah Doughty*

Carnivore

You feasted on my carrion—
a meal perfectly prepared
for a savage beast
with an appetite
only my broken soul
could satisfy.

—*Allison Theresa*

Don't
tell me
you love
the rain

when you
don't stay
to watch
her dry

after
she's fallen
for you.

—*Lauren Eden*

Each and every one of us has
a beast imprisoned inside.
The tragedy of man happens when
he unleashes the beast
and imprisons the man.

—*Daniel Saint*

Maybe just maybe
your soulmate is nothing more
than a reflection of yourself,
teaching you to love every perfect
hard to reach imperfection of you.
Because if you can love someone in spite
of theirs, why not yours.

—*a.c.sparks*

As I Lay Dying

I am not the budding flower on the tree you sit under.
I am not the sweet fruit that you savor
on a summer afternoon.
I am not the many leaves that wither away in the cold.
I am the roots—
running deeper, stronger,
firmly holding every branch,
every fruit, every leaf together.
I am what you cannot see,
yet I am a simple truth,
infusing life in the complexities.
I am what nurtures.
I am the foundations of what you seek.
I exist to create.

—*Paradox & Metaphors*

Anger is a mask
that I have grown to
wear a little too well.

—*Kate Foster*

Dear Anger,

You are sadness turned inward.
Take the balm of forgiveness
and apply it over your heart.

Love,
Your Spirit

—*Simi Fromen*

With the sun rising at my back
and dark skies ahead,
I drove into the storm
just to see what colors
might lay beyond.
I took the toll roads,
and paid my fair share.
The rain starts to roar,
crashing on the roof
of this gunmetal car.
So I hit the gas,
just to make it last.
My chest carries an anchor
hanging from a rope in my mind
knotted together with heartstrings
but it's full of mud
it's wrapped in thorns
it's weighed down by the guilt
of love lost along the way
And my cinder block toes slow
me down
on this long road home
to something that was nothing
and the fire that died within.

—*Unrulywords*

How Women Get Burned

I'm an abandoned house,
looted and ransacked
vandalized, burned.

Choking on ash.
No exceptions to your
scorched Earth policy.

Turn around.
Do you think you're the first
man to light me on fire?

Years ago, covered in dust,
dilapidated, divorced, decaying.
This was how you found me.

—*Emilija Blum*

Oxymoronic Love

This is the loudest silence I have ever heard.
Your absence is the strongest presence I have ever felt,
and this hatred has got to be the realest love
that ever existed.

—*Dru Anthony*

As I Lay Dying

Pull for push
You into me
Up against the wall
As we tear them down
Tell me the things
Within your head
I want to hear
What you hold
Within long hard kisses
Reaching our souls
Let's taste the passion
Nibbling at our necks
With our hands to hold
Wrapping around each other
Pushing into the pull

—*Joshua Ryan Stewart*

My computer keeps trying,
over and over,
to capitalize the letter *i*.

(Maybe that's our problem.)

—*Jef Joslin*

I'm a woman of strength—
comfortable in my skin,
lost in my thoughts,
and found in my words,

always holding my heart
but never my tongue.

—*Yasmin A. Gomez*

Some nights I lie awake with this ache
in my chest where your head
would've been as our words lingered
in the darkness.

Though you let the weight of you
fall on me, it still felt light,
like my fingers as they grazed
up and down your back—
easy, like the I love you's
I whispered into your hair.

The part I miss most were the moments
when you'd drum your fingers
along my chest and smile—
how I'd feel your happiness
against my skin.

I know the night will end
and I'll see you again,
but any moment without you
is too long for me.

—*Daren Colbert*

Beliefs

I believe in contradicting myself.
In proving myself wrong as often as
I prove myself right.
I believe in making mistakes
Until the lesson sticks
Or the error loses its appeal.
I believe in energy.
In manifesting it.
In carving out the people and situations
That drink it from me.
I believe in intention.
In being mindful of what it is.
In getting behind the tongue
Of the intention of others'.
I believe in intimacy.
In unadulterated communication.
In holding a gaze and in holding a hand.
I believe in gratitude.
In acknowledging all the goodness, the love.
In knowing letting go is an act of grace.

I believe in allowing myself.
I believe in denying myself.

I believe in the power and the delicacy of words.
In how important they are to get right (honesty, honestly).
In how easily they can cause misdirection (they're known
to pretty themselves up).
I believe in kindness.
In its power and its contagiousness.
In how it needs to come with a backbone and an antenna.

I believe in being comfortable.
In being myself.
In understanding what that means.

—*J. Bird*

She leaves with her spirit still intact.
No longer is it pinned
to the wall of her lover.
Too many times it has been used
for other things
besides love.
Now it's hers again to wear with pride.

—*Zachry K. Douglas*

Autopsy

Repairing my father's house I saw the window trim
come loose from the wall outside. Dead wood
from too much rain and humidity; tall trees
blocked sunlight, moisture filled its pores.

I set the tools down moved the ladder underneath
and climbed up to assess the damage; an old wound,
nails rusted through, only flesh held it together.
I ripped it off; blood dripped down my arms.

My hands scraped away skin to uncover the dermis;
bone-dry panels, humming air circulation, running water,
electricity, steady cadences. Leaned back on the rung, I
paused.

Gutters sagged from brown wet leaves—
patches of roof tile layered with moss.
I watched cardinals peck seeds from a feeder
on the porch; cracked shells and open hearts.

I looked up at the trees—limbs rigor mortis—
then called a service to cut them down.

—*Chase Maser*

As I Lay Dying

Do not reduce yourself
to anything less than
who you are meant to be,
so that your heart will not engulf people
who are not meant to survive
within its vastness.

The unworthy may drown,
but the worthy will learn how to swim.

—*Emina Gašpar Vrana*

Bear.

Toward the forbidden
to the signs of the prisoned
woven salts rest;
undying.

As drips take
to the rising waters of time,
your thoughts sail
through the air to new heights.

So I'll take your weight
and burn my own
upon this everyday emery
that tremors across
true luster.

—*A. Kelman*

Novel Romance

As much as you want to be my endless novel,
I have a feeling you will be the subtle differences
between my confessions and my regrets—
the once promising, crumbled pieces of paper
by the waste bin.
Long stories were never my strong suit.

—*Allison Theresa*

I used to be straight, fragile,
a package to handle with caution.
I bowed my spine to the feet of men
who never wanted me to rise higher than hip bones.
Then I broke, cracked my spine, and was forced to bend.
Now I am curves, zigzags, open, and flexible—
free to dodge bullets that prey upon the weak.
I am proud of my breaking—my bending of bones—
for it led me to mountains with strength at their peaks.

—*Raquel Franco*

a queen isn't arrogant.
a queen is self-confident.

—*Adrian Michael Green*

Come back to me.
Come back when you have nothing left
because right now I see you holding onto
that shred of what you call pride—
I call it ego, and they'd call it bravery.
But you are not brave.
You should call it a day,
but you are holding on to this notion that
you are, in some way, like everyone else,
just another person on this planet
who can kill themselves slowly
in moderation.
Such a thing does not exist.
It is—and will be—engraved on tombstones
up one side and down the other
of this long road home.
When you get there, give it up. All of it.
All of the bullshit screaming that
you need a glimpse of Heaven bathed in booze
in order to wash yourself in the sweet light
of recognition.
So come back to me.
But come back to me when you have nothing.

—*The Poetry Bandit*

As I Lay Dying

I have learned that I am a delicacy
and that one day someone will
whisper my name under their breath
just to savor my acquired taste.

—*Dru Anthony*

The stars will only ever be
a mild-mannered backdrop
to your beautifully reckless
midnight silhouette.

—*Kristina Fanning*

Humans are selfish beings.
We are centered on ourselves.
We crave attention.
We do good to feel good.
We pat ourselves on the back
and pout when we are not recognized
for our "selflessness."
We even love selfishly,
expecting the same love we give,
demanding it,
with the mindset that we deserve it.
What makes us so special?
Aren't we all broken, messed up souls
wandering through life,
pretending we have the answers?
So, love others with no expectations,
prerequisites, clauses, or conditions.
Give without the desire to be noticed
and applauded.
Change the world
because the world needs us
to look outside of ourselves.

Smile because the sun is shining
or because the rain falling on your
face makes you feel alive.

—*Rose C.L.*

I am savage,
wind
and wild hair.
No apologies.
Free.
Protector,
with gritted teeth,
holding on
to all I deserve.

—*Raquel Franco*

Get lonely.
Get so lonely your teeth rattle with it.
In the emptiness you will find beauty.
You will find yourself
Soft and gentle. Dewy with hope.

—*Salma El-Wardany*

she's the kind of queen
that knows her crown
isn't on her head but
in her soul.

—*Adrian Michael Green*

The Sun Also Rises

Reach.
Never stop reaching.
When you think there is nothing left to grab,
there is always more.
The universe is infinite and still unfolding,
and even as you see creation undone,
it is all the while birthing something new,
something further,
something reachable.

—*Analog de Lēon*

Courage, dear heart.
We've had our book burned before,
and each time we write it over,
it just keeps getting better and better.

—*The Poetry Bandit*

we were busy
dancing and crying.
sticking our fingers
into the empty spaces
in our chests and talking
about all the ways
we could fill them.

and life didn't hurt so much then.

and we were happy enough.

and it was precious.

—*anna corniffe*

The Sun Also Rises

It amazes me that after every winter—
the bitter cold and deep freeze—
that life returns with spring.

The flowers blossom, the birds sing,
and trees stretch their limbs,
reaching toward the sun again.

So if all the world can die once a year
and come back to tell the tale,
then we can awaken from the darkest despair,
and find a way to love again.

—*Madalyn Beck*

Mettle

Still I survive.
Even when you grind my head into the dirt.
Even when you whisper in my ear
to keep my eyes wide at night.
Still I survive.

—*Dave Wise*

Fulfillment is not so much about being at the peak.
It's about looking at your blistered and calloused
hands and feet,
knowing that you climbed
that goddamned mountain bare.

—*Daniel Saint*

Never underestimate the weight of a
pebble by its size, it still hurts.
Neither a drop of water by its quantity,
it can easily drown you.
Nor an ember from a long-dead fire,
it will still set a forest ablaze.
Or a simple transgressing crack,
which can cause colossal devastation along its path.
Small things are easily overlooked.
Never let them pass you by so easily.
They can have a vast and great turning effect in
your life, without you even realizing.
Appreciate the little things too.

—*Salman Bharadia*

Allow hope to bloom like spring daffodils—
the harbinger of magnificent change,
the testimony of beholding beauty,
the inevitable arrival of newness,
the end to a cold dullness.

Wear hope like a spring season.
After a morbid winter, it must arrive.

—*Paradox & Metaphors*

Flower Child

It's easy for a flower to bloom
while feeding off the rays of the sun,
but a wildflower that is able to flourish
in the light of the moon and stars, through the cold dirt,
brings me rays of courage, hope of perseverance.
If something so fragile
could brave the darkness and survive,
then maybe so can I.

—*Sica Saccone*

THE SUN ALSO RISES

holes in fences,
cracks in walls,
that's all I can offer, love.
i've been building for so long.
my chest—
my barricades—
could you break them down?
i'm ready to meet you,
meet you on that soft,
soft ground.

—*Jess Adams*

No one should live in a world
where their hearts keep the same steady rhythm.
Live breathless.

—*H. Christoffersen*

Be inspired by truth
Invigorated with what you have
Excited to play the part of you,
And you might just live
Happily ever after.
After all,
A fairytale is just another story told . . .
Until you decide to make it yours.

—*Krystal Lorraine*

your heart is only as
fragile as you let it be.
rip it out of your
chest and let the
world see. showing
people that you feel
something only makes
you stronger. and one
day, someone will come
along and love you, not
just for the way you
shine, but for the
scratches in your
armor. especially
the ones that
run the deepest.

—*Zack Grey*

Vox Populi

Don't tell me futile words,
of paperweight sentiments and smokescreen promises.
For my wounds were licked clean by your words, by your
healing tongue.

In the dead of night, I can still hear you
as if my scars are gently whispering,
"You are so much more than that."

—*Brittin Oakman*

I have found no other resting place for my weary heart
except within the deep grooves
of carefully chosen words
scribed here in this book of hopes.

The paper rips and cries
as I tear through years of painful memories.
The words burn through thin layers of earth,
as thoughts burn through thin layers of life.

Writing it all down
in hopes of traveling through the thick of it all
to a place where the paper won't hurt as bad as I do.

—*Allison Theresa*

One of the most challenging
things in life is learning
how to be still.

—*Jef Joslin*

For days gone by and rocket ships
lost in the flurry of our flawed universe.
For black holes and dead ends,
you will always be the beacon calling me home.
My north star in a sky of falling ones.

—*J. L. Wyman*

people spend so many nights
running their fingers through their past.
kinking their necks from looking back,
trying to make fleeting moments last and last,
longer than they're written to.
and all that while, the present is happening,
morphing into past,
and they're missing the view.

—*Cobie Kendra*

Some days I am larger than
the flesh and bones that carry me.
Other days I am smaller than
the pores that lay within this skin.
The figure that stands before you
is not a testament of my true size.
I am not to be judged by eyes alone.

—*Raquel Franco*

Insatiable

If you knew
How my mind would bend
Like refracting light
To include you
In every thought,
You would think me
Tormented by your love.

If you kncw
How my fingers would separate,
How they would reach out
In the anticipation of
Meeting your hand,
You would think me
Starved for your love.

If you knew how
My eyes would dilate,
How they would dance
In their captivation,
You would think me
Beguiled by your love.

In truth,
I am them all
When it comes to you.

I am insatiable.
I am insatiable
I am insatiable.

—*J. Bird*

Every blood vessel in these tired, red eyes
yearns for the same thing
that they have since the beginning.
I still have hope that you can see that.
Some people will call it delusion,
and I'm okay with this.
I hold that kind of expectation close
because it's the only way I know how to show loyalty—
even when the odds are against me.

—*Adan Portwood*

I don't mind the mirror,
I see hope in my reflection.

—*M. FireChild*

you, with your bruised heart
and defeated mind
who chooses to rise
with vulnerability and tenderness
as your armor.

you, with the unbreakable will
to overcome the hurt,
put fear aside
and still love.

you are the brave one.

—*E.G. Cress*

i have been loved before but you
can't tell when you first look at me

most people don't like to talk
about the times that they've lost

but you're my favorite story to tell at parties

if you asked me to describe the color hazel
i would say it looks a lot like
being left without an explanation

it was the middle of the night
when you put my hands to my sides
and told me i should stop breaking mirrors

and start practicing forgiveness.

—*s.stepp*

Rejoice in suffering,
and trust in what you cannot yet see clearly.
Believe that the outcome is sweeter
than honey in your mouth.
Darling, don't give up just yet.
You're almost there. You deserve it . . .
deserve to live in peace and experience true happiness.
That's what you were made for.
So for now, give it another go.
Every new tomorrow, give it another go.

—*Soeline Bosari*

Despite blackening skies
and sullen clouds,
I shall braid colors into my hair,
Swallow sunsets for breakfast,
And slide stars under my eyelids,
For despite blackened skies
and sullen clouds,
I choose to see the rainbow.

—*Sarah Janabi*

Made for You

I want to steal the roses off your lips
and place them to your ear,
so that you might stop and listen
to your own blooming.
You are divine
and purposeful
and real.
So, angel, stop worrying.
Keep your head up to those streaking, purple night skies.
Somebody, somewhere was made for you.
And when you wish upon the stars,
know that your love is likely wishing upon them too.

—*Michael Fawaz*

THE SUN ALSO RISES

It's a choice.
It's a choice to choose light,
to forsake the weight of our scars,
to weave pain into a tapestry of warmth
for crueler days.
The choice is terrifyingly full of promise.
The choice is yours.

You
are light.

—*Brittin Oakman*

this clock didn't seem to have numbers.
time was neither moving nor still.

the sun rose and set from a horizon i once imagined,
but never tried to look for.

i woke up last sunday with a fist full of suns in my hand
and unspoken prayers huddled beside my pillow.

i've been asleep all along.

—*israa ismaeil*

No shiny ball in the sky
could ever compare to your spirit.
Stars sputter, falter, and die.
Too often, what we see is already gone.
But you are a glorious, living, breathing soul.
In your hands is the power to master fate.
In your heart and your mind
is the key to unlock any door
no matter how it locks.
Oh, beautiful human,
I know that the dark days are heavy,
but know that your purpose is to shine
brighter than any rhinestone glittering across the sky.

—*Dave Wise*

If anyone ever asks me,
I won't say I wasted any time
while I indulged in building a life with you.
And if they wonder why it came to an end,
I'll simply tell them how I was thankful
enough to grow as a person alongside you.
Even if our roots weren't
growing in the same direction,
at least we grew.

—*H. Christoffersen*

Luring Wisdom

Our egos yell at us
to be impenetrable
and dignified.
Quiet it.
Its roar scares away wisdom.
Attract wisdom
with the sap of
weakness,
vulnerability,
transparency.
There's much sweetness
in these things.

Wisdom begins
when our quest
for perfection
ends.

—*N. Wong*

He found me cradled
In the embrace of mountains
Nestled in my untainted nirvana.
Feral, he calls me.
"Wildflower," he whispers against raw lips.
He is the sun;
A fixed point in my eternal horizon.
I trace the flames
That flicker beneath his skin,
And coax them into mine.
I am unapologetically his;
Wholly and wildly contained.
Who are you, all that I long for?
What else is life but eternity in your presence?
To be loved in the wild,
To love ferociously—
Two, no more.
One; we are one.

—*Marilyn Carp*

You, with the amaretto eyes
and lips of refreshing candor;
you, move like silent letters—
the kind people trip over
just trying to catch
but still end up
mispronouncing.
You, are a reliquary of scars
living in a world of your own,
and I—
I only hope
I'm not just passing through.

—*Rachel Kay*

I collect my mistakes like little seeds of knowledge,
plant them within the walls of my heart,
and watch myself grow.

—*Cindy Cherie*

The day I changed all my pain
into something beautiful,
I was reborn.

All my past turned into dust,
and I understood I could start again
with flowers in my hair.

—*Ariadna Blanco*

When will we learn not to search for ourselves
in other people,
when the only place we can truly find ourselves
is within?

—*Emina Gašpar-Vrana*

She stands tall and proud,
amongst perfect pieces,
a broken thing.
Behind the loud smiles,
stifled tears she often blinks.
Through metamorphosing pain,
to this blurring hope
she hopelessly clings:
without the agony of change
confined cocoons
simply never get wings.

—*Nazish Akhtar*

Motivated by
love or hate
they'll try to pull
or push you away
from who you are.
Don't break.
Don't even sway.
With steadfast resolve
occupy that space
that belongs to you
and only you.
They can join you there
or they can run away.

—*J. Warren Welch*

Stay From the Path

The greatest tragedy in life
is to believe yourself a failure
because you do not follow the path
that society demands you march.

—*Daniel Walsh*

And within her wild moments
she thought less about him
and more about loving herself,
her life,
her freedom.

—*Yasmin A. Gomez*

And so I wander
In my once-cherished paradise,
With memories that both warm
And haunt me.
I wander,
With nothing but my broken thoughts.
Waiting for dawn,
With fingers outstretched for sunlight.
His voice carries on the wind,
Accompanying the promise
Of a much-welcomed thunderstorm.
Love itself had not wronged me.
It gave me hope,
And reminded me;
Love in its entirety
Would always
Push me ever forward.

—*Marilyn Carp*

If life is the religion, then children are truly the martyrs.
The "old and wise" hammer in the nails
with every passing year
until they suffer just as their fathers did,
until they are bitter and cold
like the timeless ones before them.

If only we can keep them from that.
If only we can plant trees instead of briars.
If only we can allow them to grow to touch the sun
rather than stunt them in their spring.

—*Dave Wise*

There are times when emotions can be flooding.
The mind becomes lathered in beauty and pain,
excitement and sorrow.

This is what comes
when windows close and doors open.
The darkness throws punches,
but the light will overcome.

—*Raquel Franco*

We watch the ocean's whispered winds
buffet the seagulls way up high,
and we wonder why we can't learn to love life's lessons,
which push and pull us along
in quite the same way these birds love
the wind.

—*Rose C.L.*

The Sun Also Rises

Fall has always been my favorite time,
watching the trees outside my window.
I see myself in the leaves.

How they seem to be lost,
scattered,
and dying only to be reborn,
new and green.

How the trees lose their color
only to gain new and vibrant shades.

Change is always coming,
and it is nothing to be feared.
Dead leaves are not the end of a tree,
they're just another beginning.

So, I watch the trees outside my window,
and I hold on.

—*Michael Layao*

Look Homeward, Angel

i do not want to wear the world on the back
of my hands because then you might believe
i know everything and maybe i would, too.
instead, i will take time learning how to read
and discover you in pieces, because so often
when we get everything all at once
it is taken away just as fast.

what we build could be a table for two, or four, or
maybe even nothing, but the thing that matters most
is that our palms are not left empty.
when they are filled with every layer
we have lived and loved,
our arms will know it was worth the weight.

i will not walk with fists at my side
because when my hands are out and open
it is easier to catch the things that may fall,

like stars,
the rain
and you.

—*Wilder*

LOOK HOMEWARD, ANGEL

we wear our histories
heavy on our backs.

it's time i unpacked
my spine,

stood up straight
and moved on.

—*Jess Adams*

We are our own masterpiece,
our scars painted like graffiti
on the skeleton that carries us.

—*M. FireChild*

Rock Solid

Life weighs one thousand pounds,
but it feels like more.
And while my elbows break and my knees buckle,
I wonder how much more pressure I can take
before I crack
or turn into a diamond.

—*Gabriel Sage*

Faerytale

As the years elapsed,
her pain became her happiness,
her suffering her strength,
and her scars her wisdom.

Her passion became incorrigible
and she burned for so much more
than to merely subsist.

The echoing silence that once screamed her name
now beckoned her stay
as she began to crave existence
and yearn for nothing less than the remarkable.

She was reborn—brutally and unapologetically—
and she no longer had need of a hero,
for she had become her own savior
in the creases of her mind—
a heroine in her own right.

—*Becca Lee*

Wisdom can't be bought.
It must be found.
It must be earned.
It's the beautiful cuts
on our soles
from where our feet meet the earth.
The blood we bleed,
those scarlet footsteps that we leave,
it's the way that we must lead.
That's the way we must lead.

—*Jess Adams*

The corrosion I feel in my bones as the years creep by
comforts me in quite a peculiar way.
My beginning gives way to the closing chapters,
and there's something exciting about ending,
whether happy or otherwise . . .
for to end
means to have the opportunity of beginning anew
down a different avenue.
I'm aware that one day the final ending will be upon me,
but even then I anticipate a future of forever.

—*Rose C.L.*

Hatch

This is not your heart breaking, my darling.
This is your heart hatching,
shedding the shell of who you once were.
This is your rebirth.

— *T. Weiss*

Like a butterfly testing its wings for the first time,
she prepares herself for the initial flight of her life.
In becoming who she is, she had to shed who she was
for the betterment of her spirit.

Now she's an adventure waiting to happen,
and the stars are now home.

—*Zachry K. Douglas*

Bend the ladders
of your ribs.
Release your heart
from the inside out.

—*Raquel Franco*

Evanescence

Scarlet hues streaked the horizon
as the girl in the red dress
faded from sight.

"Wait!" he called,
clutching nothing but a glass slipper
to remember her by.

"How shall I find you?"

His reply came as a distant song,
drifting in the wind,
painting picture-perfect evanescence
across the midnight sky.

"When I find myself, I'll let you know."

—*Cindy Cherie*

Pain, in all its madness, is a potent and relentless ally. Don't look at it with fear. Consider it the soil and you are a sprouting tree. Consider it wind and you are a potential hurricane. With pain, you'll grow stronger and stronger, every time it hurts.

—*a.r.lucas*

learn to love the moments
between destinations,
the quiet moments with yourself,
the slow moments when life
seems to be waiting to give you
your next instruction;

trust that you're preparing
for the next stage of your life,
and be ready when the next door opens,
and it's time to walk inside.

—*Mark Anthony*

Spring in Every Season

Sometimes the simple things take me by surprise.

The Reveille
the sparrow sings.
Our child nursing.
Hazel fractals in your eyes.

The joys of spring, of new life, of rebirth!

The seasons may change with their own timing,
but in my mind I'll always find the simple surprises
spring is known to bring.

—*C. Noel*

Gratefulness

The fullness of one breath,
fully lived.

—*Fiorella Giordano*

The facade of bravado falls
with my clothing to the floor,
with my makeup down the drain,
with the cold water
every night before I sleep.

I am stripped naked of my masks and pride—
all flaws exposed, even the ones I keep inside.

The mirror reveals them to my searching eyes.
Everyone should stand naked daily
because we are human, we are broken,
and we are beautiful.

—*Rose C.L.*

I let myself burn deep within my bones.
Nothing remains but ashes.
I am waiting for the smoke to settle,
and once the skies clear,
I will emerge from the smoldering rubble
reborn,
free of the chains with which I once bound myself,
a sinful distraction to pass the time.
Now I am naked, basking in my truth.
All that's left of the past are my stories—
words I once whispered
with hopes that someone would hear me.
I was lost for so long in a world promising me love.
I am leaving it behind to discover the fire
igniting within me.

—*Jessica Michelle*

I am a strange and wild thing.
I dance with no music and talk to silence,
and I regret nothing.

—*Ariadna Blanco*

Women Within

Every experience introduces me
to another woman, and all of these women
wear my face—
they are all mine.

So, knowing you
was not a waste of time.
Because of you, I met a very strong me.
She came into my body and
taught me
to be kind in the face of cruelty,
to forgive the undeserving,
to sacrifice in the name of hope,
and persist when met with defiance.

This woman taught me suppleness
in the midst of thorniness,
and I love her for this.
You're gone now, and a new woman
wearing my face taps me on the shoulder.
She is just as strong as the last,
but she is wise.

Again I open my ribs and wave her in.
From her, I'm learning
about my worth and my boundaries.
But most importantly, she is teaching me
to always heed any woman
within me if she tells me
something is amiss.

—*N. Wong*

Allow yourself to experience the beauty
of forgiveness and the grace of change.
Allow yourself to move on, to let go.

—*Paradox & Metaphors*

I've fallen in love with the absence of your heartbeat.
The silence is a peaceful reminder that I deserve more.

—*H. Christoffersen*

He sends me love songs
In my sleep
He lies awake
But dreams of me.
The pain of absence
Lodged so deep
We feel the ache
Concurrently.
And while he sleeps
Again I rise
And face the morning
On my own
A tender longing for the jones
My heart's injected
To the bone.
And while he breathes
I find my way
Hold fast to
Every curve and bend
So he can breathe
Into my lungs
And one plus one
Is two again.

—*r.z. joyce*

Sometimes all you can do is laugh,
empty your pockets and hands,
run into the street giddy like a madman,
and throw a finger to the world.

—*A.R. Asher*

I scoured the earth incessantly,
to find the valiant love I craved.
I deviated from my path,
to the unknown that I braved.
I seek a love that grips me,
through every waking night,
and amends all my wrongs,
til they eventually feel right.
A love that will invest,
in my ever-changing dreams,
and that will calm the panic attacks,
of my many silent screams.
A love that will not hesitate,
to haul my heavy pain,
and one I can surely trust,
to never leave or wane.
I reflected upon the path,
carved throughout my solo quest,
and the wounds I have healed,
from the strength of my own press;
the obstacles I conquered,
my persistence advanced me through;
and determination drove me,
down a road I never knew.
When my conviction finally struck me,
my search needn't be prolonged,
as the valiant love I was looking for,
lived inside me all along.

—Vivi Dale

I found a home in the arms of strangers.
We dance with bare feet,
Chest-to-chest
Under the light of the moon.
Laughing away our sanity
And howling at the moon.
Wildlings,
Content with our lack of direction.
And now, here we lie;
Beneath the skin of stars,
Tasting the stories that fall from their lips.
Restless oceans surround us here,
As we inhale our dreams.
Pain, with nothing to feed on, does not thrive here.
And we know;
We are finally home.

—*Marilyn Carp*

I run my fingers along
the string of a guitar
I cannot play—the sound
could be beautiful, if I
strummed it differently.

I think maybe I have liked
the things that are just
out of reach—because
to yearn is different than
to grieve.

—*Kristen Laura Costa*

Sometimes we become addicted to our trauma.
It both weakens and strengthens us,
but we must let go.
It is liberating—but also a bit sad—
to relinquish the power it's given us
to make excuses, to cry, to retreat, and to lash out.

It's become a part of us.

Let go of the pain so you may regain your true strength.

—*Allison Theresa*

In the wake of you I saw hell.
I traveled seven circles deep inside myself.
It wasn't until the bottom,
the very depths,
the breaking point,
that I found traces of life.
Littered on the ground
were fragments of who I used to be
and reminders of
who I could be again.
I collected the pieces in my tired hands
and counted;
not enough to live,
no,
but enough to start my resurrection.
I needed to learn how to live again
and losing everything
was my greatest lesson.

—*Michael Layao*

Dearest,
when life's trials seem to overwhelm you
and peace is far from your heart,
when your soul becomes too weary
and your mind is drowning in burdensome thoughts,
please know that an anchor of strength
can be found in the arms of love.

—*Soeline Bosari*

No single soul walking this gritty earth
is ever meant to remain seamless.
Our edges, flaws, indications, and interruptions,
free us from being a carbon copy.
That's the purest freedom of all.

—*Kate Foster*

Silence

It's really quiet sometimes.
I need it, the silence.
At times I need to be alone with it.
When it is all too real, when I am
overwhelmed by life, I seek it out.

I don't know if it helps,
but it is there, and for a time
that is all that matters.

—*Daniel Walsh*

A crushed reed.
A damaged petal.
My garden is a lost secret and a lost cause to most.
But not to you.
You see vibrancy and life in what others dismissed
as sparse and meager.
With your masterful skills,
you gently pull the weeds from my red, beating heart.
You toil in the sun and work my soul
with the tenderness of an experienced gardener.
You grow from me a sophisticated vine.
A willow tree.
An olive branch.
Now paradise sprouts amongst soil
that is rich with forgiveness.
Let mercy rain down on me.
Let your love water my recovery.

—*J. L. Wyman*

Ethereal

Too often are we afraid to fall,
mistaking mortality as our curse.

My dear, when will you learn that to bleed
is the greatest of gifts?

For humanity knows the bounds of life and loss
which privileges us to love as no angel,
hallowed or forsaken, may know.

So before you renounce the fragile flesh upon you,
discover the truth in the blood
licked from your wounds . . .
for the most vital lessons are learned in the falls,
and your greatest wisdom is born from the depths
of your surmounted despair.

Your greatest strength lies in welcome imperfections.

—*Becca Lee*

as drowning turns to life
as songs turn to breath
waves no longer pummel
another mermaid cheats death

maybe the magic is all we need
to live without hindrance
of what normality sees.

—*C. Churchill*

She is a magnificent representation of
winning wars with only hope holding her spirit together
and determination painted on her lips.

—*Kayil Crow*

When we're surrounded by chaos, we find ways to
make peace against the turbulence once we find
ourselves between life's hectic pace,
in the pockets of stillness.
It's in our nature to revel in chaos, the frequencies
of agitation still resonate within us no matter how
much we think we're above it. We're part of it.
I've learned some of my deepest lessons immersed
in the chaos. But it's also worn me down a few
times. So my creativity is sparked by what lives
between the chaos and peace. Both inside and out.

—*dáeizm*

What are peaks and valleys when you
have someone who kisses your
forehead at night and holds your hand
in the car?

—*Ryan Hennessy*

If you have
no desire
to get back up,
then there was
no point in
being
knocked down.

—*Andrew Durst*

My scars are sketching
the bridge to my strength
as my courage leads the way.

—*M. FireChild*

we lie tonight
as we have lain
with any lover,
who has ever
proved us a phoenix.

hopes undressed; we are carried
in the palm
of a new year's tender hand.

may it never strike in malice.

it is tonight, in hope
and in love,
that we are reborn.

—*Jess Adams*

I did not rise because I am strong.
I rose because I have a purpose
stronger than all of my weaknesses.

—*Dru Anthony*

Love will endure the silence,
but you have to be willing to scream.

—*Vivi Dale*

I stood there, waiting for proof—
proof that I could survive,
proof that I would resurface from the rubble
beneath which I buried myself.
I was waiting for a sign from the heavens—
a sign that I would find the strength
to get through this hell.
And through all the time I spent waiting,
I made it.

—*Jessica Michelle*

She grew tired of chasing storms,
so she became one.
And now they chase after her.

—*Adrian Michael Green*

We are a restless bunch
born of the same stardust as royalty.
We are all noble creatures of infinite light,
yet we have buried our inheritance in mud bricks
that now rise up around every corner of our hearts.

In this land of broken dreams,
I will no longer stand watchman
to an empty tower.
I will use my hands to deconstruct
all that my mistakes
and my regrets have built around me.

I will take back my inheritance,
hidden in the bricks,
and when I have carved a hole in the wall
I will step out into the world of tomorrow,
a blank canvas stitched in light and confidence.

We deconstruct our walls
as we learn to love ourselves.

—*Analog de Lēon*

I keep reaching for something
Too tall for me
Damn these roots
That hold me here
Digging into the ground
The soil
The black of your skin
The promises you wouldn't give
Keeping me on earth
When I was made for more
When I was made
For a higher love

—*Heidi Kidd*

She undresses her wounds,
stripping to vulnerability,
leaving behind anything
that does not lift her soul.

—*Simi Fromen*

Atop a mountain in the desert,
the same sun, that every soul
who ever lived beheld,
warms the still air of a new morning.
Light vibrates everything
underneath a cloudless sky,
while high desert winds pick up
and push the warm air,
ripe with energy,
toward the flat expanse below.
I, cradled in the vastness,
absorb the charged gust,
breathe the boiling breeze into my lungs,
and hold the universe inside my breath.

—*Gabriel Sage*

About the Authors

Crown Anthology is a collection by Lost Poets featuring over one hundred diverse voices from around the world, curated to be a light in the wild dark, illuminating the crown that exists in everyone.

An Open Letter to the Lost

O'Lost,

We are a lost generation of analog people living in a digital age, where truth has gone the alternative way of rumor, social good has become secondary to economic gain, beauty is defined by Photoshop, and prejudice has become the dominant voice of our generation. The silicon age of information has smothered us into paralysis, stolen our privacy, and conditioned us to line up to be the first to buy big brother.

The world has never needed voices of resistance more, voices of hope and self-love, of fresh water and empowerment. We desperately need more Bob Dylan and Maya Angelou style voices. Join us and commit your art to the resistance. Great art has purpose . . .

Sincerely from the planet Earth,

Analog de Lēon
A Moniker of Chris Purifoy

Artist Index

a.c.sparks 90, ... @a.c.sparks

Adan Portwood 70, 138. . . . . @adanportwood

Adrian Michael Green 74, 109, 116, 209 . . @adrianmichaelgreen

A.D.Woods 73 . . . . @a.d.woods

A.Kelman 106 . . . . @akscrolls

Alice Morrison 6. . . . . @alicemorrison514

Alison Malee 9, 42, 78 . . . . @alison.malee

Allison Theresa 12, 87, 107, 132, 192 . . . . @_allisontheresa_

Allison Theresa and Gabriel Sage 55

Almaz A. 53 . . . . @almazspilledink

Analog de Léon 4, 23, 43, 81, 118, 210 . . . @analog.words

Andrew Durst 35, 203 . . . . @andrewdurst

angie allen 58 . . . . @angie.l.allen

anna corniffe 120 . . . . @theannacorniffe

Anthony Desmond 16 . . . . @anthonydesmondpoetry

A.R. Asher 33, 188 . . . . @a.r.asher

Ariadna Blanco 153, 183 . . . . @voicelesswriter

a.r.lucas 177 . . . . @a.r.lucas

Becca Lee 62, 170, 198 . . . . @beccaleepoetry

Brittin Oakman 131, 145 . . . . @b.oakman

Caroline White 59 . . . . @cwpoet

C. Churchill 199 . . . . @cc_writes

Chase Maser 31, 104 . . . . @pspoets

Christopher Ferreiras 2, 60 . . . . @itscarus

Cindy Cherie 22, 152, 176 . . . . @cindycherie

Artist Index

C. Noel   37, 179 . . . . @noelsnotebook

Cobie Kendra   135 . . . . @cobiekendra

dáeizm   201 . . . . @daeizm

Daniel Saint   15, 89, 123 . . . . @daniel.saint

Daniel Walsh   19, 157, 196 . . . . @daniel.peter.walsh

Daren Colbert   100 . . . . @darencolbert

Dave Wise   122, 147, 160 . . . . @d.a.wise

Dru Anthony   96, 111, 206 . . . . @dru.anthony

E.G. Cress   140 . . . . @e.g.cress

Emilija Blum   52, 95 . . . . @emilijablum

Emina Gašpar-Vrana   69, 105, 154 . . . . @emina.gasparvrana

Erin Van Vuren   46 . . . . @papercrumbs

faraway   36 . . . . @farawaypoetry

featherdownsoul   29 . . . . @featherdownsoul

Fiorella Giordano   180 . . . . @giordano.fiorella

Gabrielle Dufrene   56 . . . . @4.26pm

Gabriel Sage   39, 48, 61, 169, 213 . . . . @gabrielsage

H. Christoffersen   128, 148, 186 . . . . . @hailey.christoffersen

Heidi Kidd   211 . . . . @heidi_the_untold

Horacio Jones   40, 82 . . . . @horaciojones

israa ismaeil   146 . . . . @iaismaeil

Jarod W.   80 . . . . @rodandrew16

J. Bird   14, 21, 49, 101, 137 . . . . @j.birdsmith

Jef Joslin   98, 133 . . . . @jeffreyscottjoslinii

Jess Adams   127, 167, 171, 205 . . . . . . @jessadamsgrams

Jessica Michelle   182, 208 . . . . @_jessie.michelle_

J. L. Wyman   71, 134, 197 . . . . @j.l.wyman

Joshua Ryan Stewart   97 . . . . @joshua_ryan_stewart

J. Warren Welch   156 . . . . @j.warren.welch

Kate Foster   44, 92, 195 . . . . @kaitlin.foster

Kayil Crow   64, 200 . . . . @rose_thorns1921

Artist Index

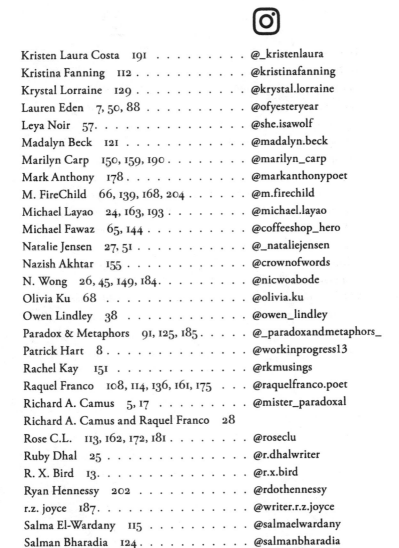

Kristen Laura Costa   191 . . . . @_kristenlaura
Kristina Fanning   112 . . . . @kristinafanning
Krystal Lorraine   129 . . . . @krystal.lorraine
Lauren Eden   7, 50, 88 . . . . @ofyesteryear
Leya Noir   57 . . . . @she.isawolf
Madalyn Beck   121 . . . . @madalyn.beck
Marilyn Carp   150, 159, 190 . . . . @marilyn_carp
Mark Anthony   178 . . . . @markanthonypoet
M. FireChild   66, 139, 168, 204 . . . . . . @m.firechild
Michael Layao   24, 163, 193 . . . . @michael.layao
Michael Fawaz   65, 144 . . . . @coffeeshop_hero
Natalie Jensen   27, 51 . . . . @_nataliejensen
Nazish Akhtar   155 . . . . @crownofwords
N. Wong   26, 45, 149, 184 . . . . @nicwoabode
Olivia Ku   68 . . . . @olivia.ku
Owen Lindley   38 . . . . @owen_lindley
Paradox & Metaphors   91, 125, 185 . . . . . @_paradoxandmetaphors_
Patrick Hart   8 . . . . @workinprogress13
Rachel Kay   151 . . . . @rkmusings
Raquel Franco   108, 114, 136, 161, 175 . . . @raquelfranco.poet
Richard A. Camus   5, 17 . . . . @mister_paradoxal
Richard A. Camus and Raquel Franco   28
Rose C.L.   113, 162, 172, 181 . . . . @roseclu
Ruby Dhal   25 . . . . @r.dhalwriter
R. X. Bird   13 . . . . @r.x.bird
Ryan Hennessy   202 . . . . @rdothennessy
r.z. joyce   187 . . . . @writer.r.z.joyce
Salma El-Wardany   115 . . . . @salmaelwardany
Salman Bharadia   124 . . . . @salmanbharadia
Sarah Doughty   86 . . . . @thesarahdoughty
Sarah Janabi   143 . . . . @immortal.thought

Artist Index

Sarah Maria   83 . . . . @sarahmariawrites

Shakespeare   *vii*

Sica Saccone   20, 30, 126 . . . . @sica.says

Simi Fromen   93, 212 . . . . @simi_fromen

S.L. Gray   34 . . . . @s.l._gray

Soeline Bosari   72, 142, 194 . . . . @wordsbysoeline

s.stepp   141 . . . . @s.stepp

stacie martin   67 . . . . @stacie.martin

The Poetry Bandit   63, 75, 110, 119 . . . . @the_poetrybandit

Topher Kearby   3, 85 . . . . @topherkearby

T. Weiss   47, 54, 173 . . . . @axiom.attic

Tyler Knott Gregson   *v* . . . .@tylerknott

Unrulywords   94 . . . . @unrulywords

Vivi Dale   11, 18, 32, 189, 207 . . . . . . @vivi.dale

Wilder   166 . . . . @wilderpoetry

Yasmin A. Gomez   99, 158 . . . . @yasmingomez.official

Zachry K. Douglas   103, 174 . . . . @zachrykdouglas

Zack Grey   130 . . . . @zackgreywrites

ACKNOWLEDGMENTS

Raise a glass . . .

This book was made possible by the tireless efforts of dedicated people and artists.

Vivi Dale, you are the backbone and the foundation of this book. More than a friend to every single person here, your perseverance and knowledge took this project to new heights.

Raquel Franco, thank you for your endless contributions. Your fingerprints are on every page.

M. FireChild, thank you for never giving up and for taking on some of the hardest challenges we faced. Every band of dreamers needs a fire child.

Sidd Long and Yasmin Gomez, thank you both for being pioneers.

To everyone else, thank you for your time, incredible dedication, and powerful words. Special thanks to: Fiorella Giordano, Cindy Cherie, Daniel Walsh, Jess Adams, Dru Anthony, Soeline Bosari, Jessica Michelle, N. Wong, Christopher Ferreiras, J. Bird, and Michael Fawaz.

Vive la Renaissance!

—Gabriel & Analog

About Lost Poets

Lost Poets is a voice of resistance and hope, cofounded by Analog de Léon and Gabriel Sage. Its books, events, and projects empower a global subculture of modern poets.

CROWN ANTHOLOGY

Andrews McMeel Publishing
a division of Andrews McMeel Universal
1130 Walnut Street, Kansas City, Missouri 64106

www.andrewsmcmeel.com

18 19 20 21 22 BVG 10 9 8 7 6 5 4 3 2 1

ISBN: 978-1-4494-9410-0

Library of Congress Control Number: 2018939581

Additional Editors: Raquel Franco and Nicole Wong
Cover illustration: Alevtina Golovina

Editor: Patty Rice
Designer, Art Director: Diane Marsh
Production Editor: Elizabeth A. Garcia
Production Manager: Cliff Koehler